This book belongs to:

_____

CUENTO
DE LUZ

To my father and to my mother,
who knits dreams with her magic ball of wool.

- Susanna Isern -

To my mother, who believes in magic.

- Nora Hilb -

The Magic Ball of Wool

Text © Susanna Isern
Illustrations © Nora Hilb
This edition © 2013 Cuento de Luz SL
Calle Claveles 10 | Urb Monteclaro | Pozuelo de Alarcón | 28223 | Madrid | Spain
www.cuentodeluz.com
Original title in Spanish: El ovillo mágico
English translation by Jon Brokenbrow

ISBN: 978-84-15619-89-5

Printed by Shanghai Chenxi Printing Co., Ltd. March 2013, print number 1353-2

FSC
www.fsc.org
MIX
Paper from
responsible sources
FSC® C007923

THE MAGIC BALL OF WOOL

Susanna Isern

Nora Hilb

X

7

The story goes that one night in the forest,
near dawn, a large ball of wool appeared
floating in the air.

Light as a balloon, the ball of wool floated
through the hedgehog's window. It was so
quiet that when it got stuck on his prickles,
the little creature didn't even stir.

At sunrise, the spider on the doorknob
(who woke up very early so that she could
get her web ready) saw the mysterious
ball of wool stuck on the hedgehog's back.
Her friend was still snoring away merrily.

"Wake up, hedgehog!" shouted the spider in a frightened voice.
"What's up?" asked the hedgehog, curling himself into a ball.
"You've got a great big ball of wool stuck on your prickles.
Can't you feel it?"

The hedgehog, who was quite used to shaking things out of his prickles, turned around in his bed, and the ball of wool fell off. He looked at it with surprise and said, "What could I do with this ball of wool?"
"Well, wool is for knitting scarves, mittens or sweaters," answered the spider from her web. "If you like, I can teach you."

The hedgehog plucked out his two longest prickles to use as knitting needles, and the spider, who was an expert, taught him how to knit.

Soon, all of the forest animals heard about the mysterious arrival of the ball of wool. And so, one by one and full of curiosity, they came to see what was happening in the hedgehog's house.

The first creature who came along was the mouse. Seeing the hedgehog enthusiastically knitting away, he said, "Good morning, hedgehog! I came to see you and your ball of wool. Could you knit something for me?"
"Of course I could, little mouse. I'll knit you a sweater."

CLICKETY-CLICK, CLICKETY-CLICK ...
a stitch here, a stitch there ...

The hedgehog knitted a tiny sweater. But just as he finished, something magical happened ...
The woolen sweater turned into a great big ball of cheese!
The mouse was overjoyed. He loved cheese more than anything else in the world!

His next visitor was the frog.

CLICKETY-CLICK, CLICKETY-CLICK ...
A stitch here, a stitch there ...

The hedgehog knitted some fancy mittens for the frog. But just as he finished, something amazing happened ...
The woolen mittens turned into a gleaming mirror!
The frog was delighted. As she was very vain, she'd always dreamed of having a mirror in which she could look at herself all day long.

His next visitor was the bear.

CLICKETY-CLICK, CLICKETY-CLICK ...
A stitch here, a stitch there ...

The hedgehog knitted a great big balaclava complete with a hole for
his friend's snout, but the cap turned into a shell in which the bear
could hear the sea!

Then along came the centipede.

CLICKETY-CLICK, CLICKETY-CLICK ...
A stitch here, a stitch there ...

This time, the hedgehog patiently knitted one hundred socks, which turned into one hundred pairs of brightly colored castanets that entertained the centipede for hours!

Then along came the snail.

CLICKETY-CLICK, CLICKETY-CLICK ...
A stitch here, a stitch there ...

The hedgehog knitted a scarf that covered the snail's shell, but it turned into a tiny scooter that could take him wherever he was going much faster than he'd ever dreamed possible.

And so, all of the animals in the forest got whatever they wanted most in the world from the hedgehog and his magic ball of wool.

One afternoon, a crab knocked on the hedgehog's door. He'd hiked
through three forests and climbed two mountains to find him.

"Hello, hedgehog! They say you've got a ball of wool and can knit things.
I've come a long, long way to ask you for a strong, long rope," said
the crab, exhausted after his journey.
"Has something happened?" asked the hedgehog, concerned by the
crab's visit.
"A huge blue whale has got stuck on the beach," explained the worried
crab. "He weighs more than two hundred tons, and we can't move him.
If he doesn't get back in the water soon ..."

The hedgehog ran off to get his two knitting prickles and the ball of wool. But all he found was a tiny piece no longer than an ant.

The magic ball of wool had run out!

The crab returned to the beach with empty claws. The hedgehog was so upset he couldn't sleep at all; he just kept thinking about the poor blue whale who'd got stuck on the beach.

News traveled fast in the forest. It was carried on the wind, and with the birds and the bees. And in the same way the animals had found out about the arrival of the ball of wool, they immediately heard the sad story of the whale.

So that night, one by one, they left the things they loved most of all outside the hedgehog's door: a big ball of cheese (now slightly nibbled), a shiny mirror, a hundred pairs of brightly colored castanets, a shell in which the sea crashed, and an itty bitty scooter ...

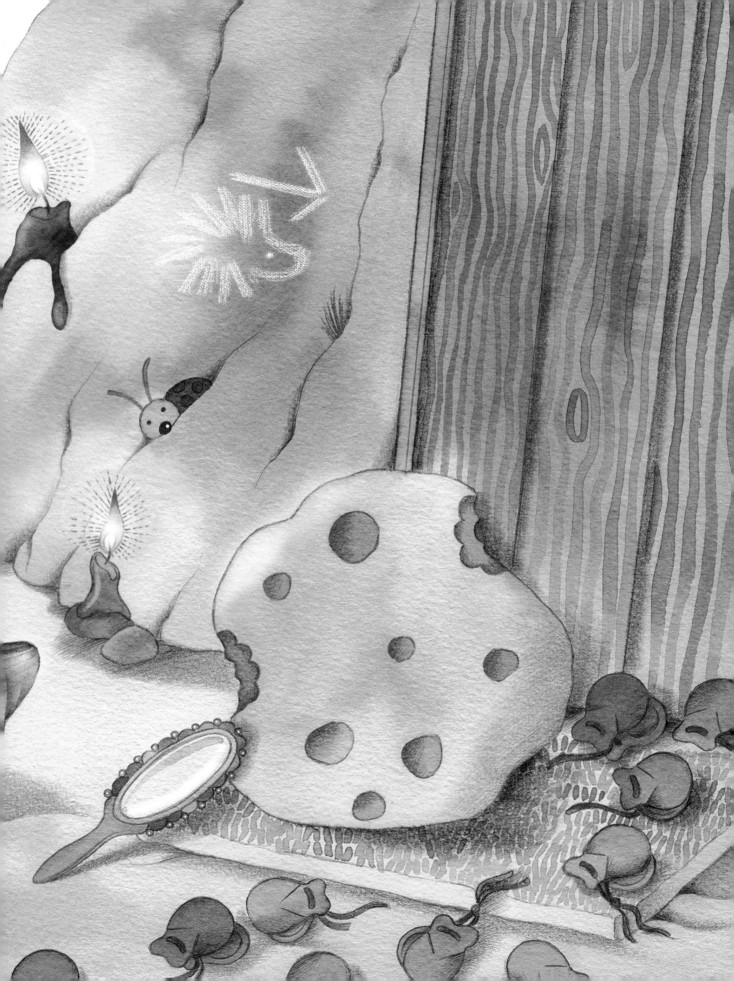

In the morning, the hedgehog saw that all of the wishes had been
returned and he understood what he had to do. The forest animals
had given up their presents to help save the blue whale. All
he had to do was pull the thread from each of them and
he would have the whole ball of wool once again.

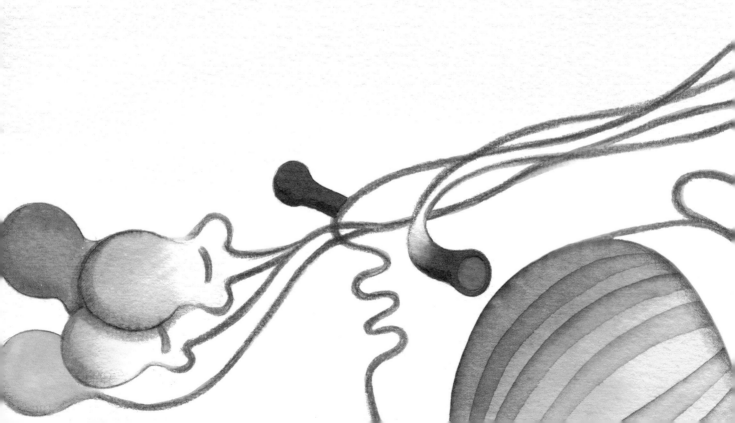

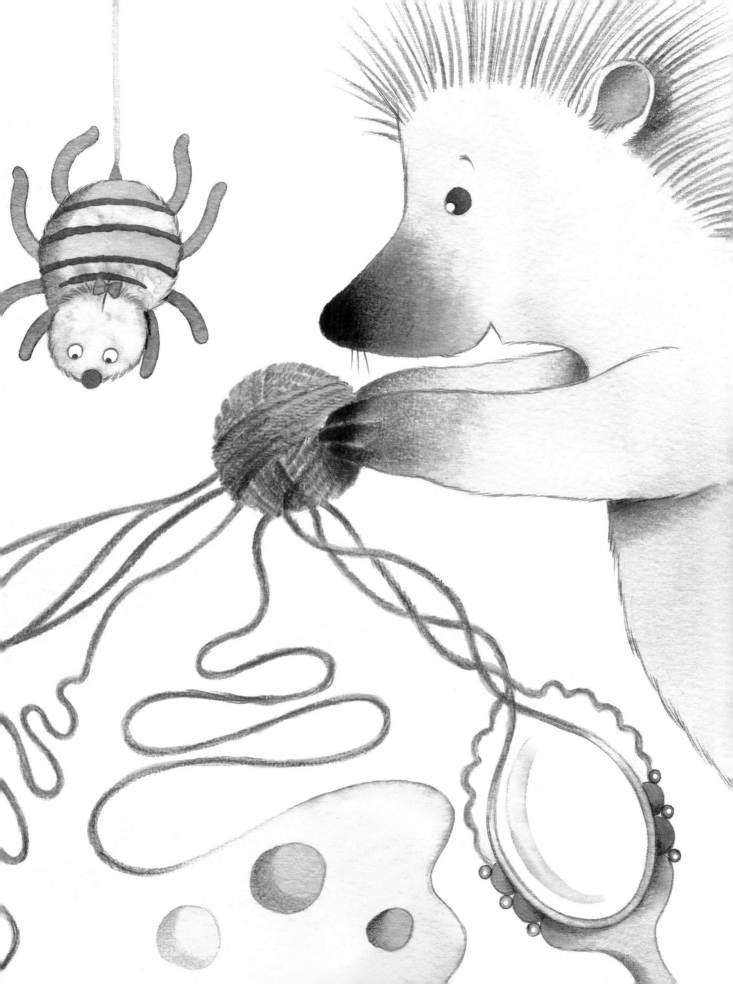

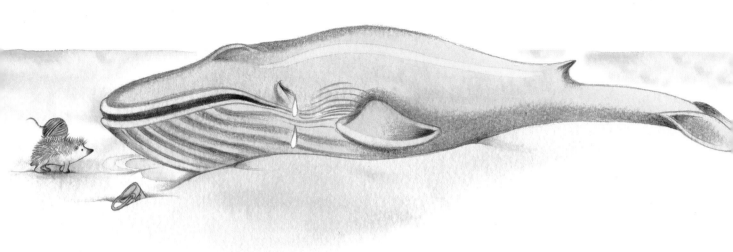

With the ball of wool stuck on his back, the hedgehog hiked through three forests and climbed two mountains, until he came to the sea and found the blue whale sobbing on the sand.

CLICKETY-CLICK, CLICKETY-CLICK ...
A stitch here, a stich there ...

The hedgehog knitted a long, strong rope. But just as he finished, something amazing and magical happened ...
The woolen rope turned into a gigantic butterfly!

The beautiful butterfly's flapping wings surrounded the hedgehog and the marine animals in a sea breeze full of hope. It opened its wings wide, wrapped them around the blue whale, and returned it to the salty water.

Each and every one of the creatures on the beach, in the water and in the air who saw this amazing sight joined the forest animals in discovering that the ball of wool was truly magical.

They say that late one night, close to dawn, an enormous,
magical ball of wool that had turned into a butterfly
flew through the sky in the forest.

Where it went is another mystery.